Melrose and Croc

FIND A SMILE

by Emma Chichester Clark

HarperCollins *Children's Books*

It was a lovely sunny day,
but something was wrong.
"What's happened?"
asked Little Green Croc.

"I've lost my smile," said Melrose.

"Well, let's go and find it then!" said Little Green Croc.

Melrose and Little Green Croc got in the car
and drove out to the country.

"But how will we find it?" asked Melrose.

"Well," said Little Green Croc,

"first, we have to run, as fast as we can...

…just like this!"

"Then we have to hop over a stream, without touching the water...

…just like this!" said Little Green Croc.

"Then we have to chase a squirrel up a tree,

just like this…

...and say hello to every cow,

just like this!" said Little Green Croc.

"Next, we find a yellow flower and smell it,"
said Little Green Croc, "just like this…

and catch a falling leaf, just like this…

...which you wear on your nose, just like this,

and walk backwards up the hill, just like this!"
said Little Green Croc.

"Then you sit in a special place and forget about everything," said Little Green Croc.

"What were we looking for?"
asked Little Green Croc.

"I can't remember!" said Melrose,
and he smiled, just like this!

First published in paperback in Great Britain by HarperCollins Children's Books in 2006

This edition published specially for Bookstart in 2007

1 3 5 7 9 10 8 6 4 2

ISBN-10: 0-00-778392-2

ISBN-13: 978-0-00-778392-2

Text and illustrations copyright © Emma Chichester Clark 2006

HarperCollins Children's Books is a division of HarperCollins Publishers Ltd.

Visit our website at: www.harpercollinschildrensbooks.co.uk

Printed and bound in Singapore

Read all the stories about Melrose and Croc

Melrose and Croc
FIND A SMILE

ISBN: 978-0-00-718241-1

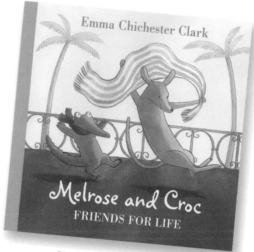

Melrose and Croc
FRIENDS FOR LIFE

ISBN: 978-0-00-718242-8

All £5.99

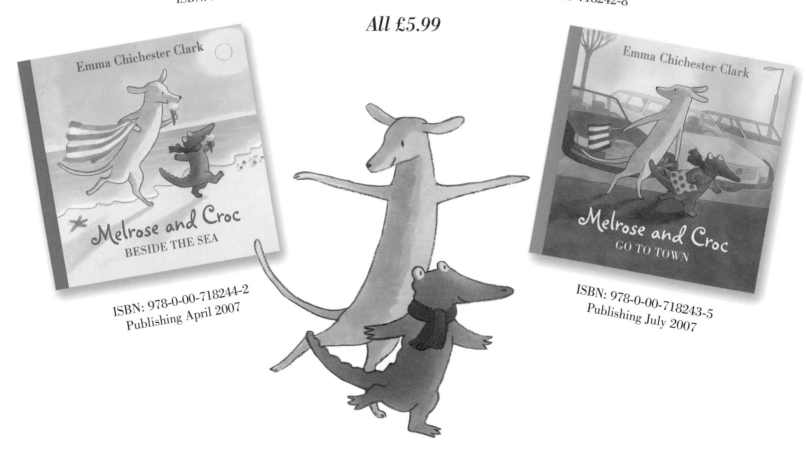

Melrose and Croc
BESIDE THE SEA

ISBN: 978-0-00-718244-2
Publishing April 2007

Melrose and Croc
GO TO TOWN

ISBN: 978-0-00-718243-5
Publishing July 2007